# Good

# Who's  Snoring?

"Good morning, who's snoring?" said Benny.

"Not I," said the sun.

"Good morning, who's snoring?" said Benny.

"Not I," barked the dog, and he jumped out of his kennel.

"Good morning, who's snoring?" said Benny.

"Not I," baaed the sheep, and she got to her feet.

"Good morning, who's snoring?" said Benny.

"Not I," grunted the pig, and he began to eat.

"Good morning, who's snoring?"
said Benny.

"Not us," said the chickens.

Benny fed the chickens.
He put the eggs in his pocket

Benny went into the house.
"Good morning, who's snoring?"
said Benny.

"Not I," said Mom,
and she put the eggs
into the pot to cook.

"Good morning, who's snoring?"
shouted Benny,
and he jumped onto the bed.

15

"I am," said Dad.
"It's Saturday!"